MY BIG FAT ZOMBIE GOLDFISH

THE FINTASTIC FISH-SITTER

To the original Sami and all the other amazing kids
in my life, especially Daniel and Charlotte.

M.O.

To my wife Hannah and son Oscar.
Love you loads!

M.J.

First published 2015 by Macmillan Children's Books,
an imprint of Pan Macmillan
a division of Macmillan Publishers Limited
20 New Wharf Road, London N1 9RR
Associated companies throughout the world
www.panmacmillan.com

ISBN: 978-1-4472-7760-6 (HB)
ISBN: 978-1-4472-7761-3 (PB)

Text copyright © Mo O'Hara 2015
Illustrations copyright © Marek Jagucki 2015

Moral rights asserted.

1 3 5 7 9 8 6 4 2

A CIP catalogue record for this book is available from the British Library.

Printed in China

MY BIG FAT ZOMBIE GOLDFISH
THE FINTASTIC FISH-SITTER

MO O'HARA   MAREK JAGUCKI

MACMILLAN CHILDREN'S BOOKS

I'm Tom and this is my best friend Pradeep who lives next door. We have a big fat zombie goldfish named Frankie.

Unfortunately, my big brother Mark has a cute but evil vampire kitten named Fang.

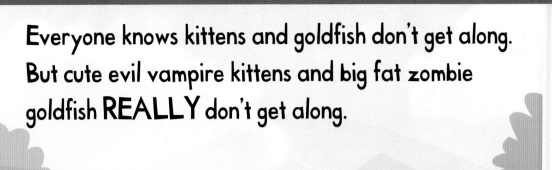

Everyone knows kittens and goldfish don't get along. But cute evil vampire kittens and big fat zombie goldfish **REALLY** don't get along.

So when we asked Pradeep's little sister Sami to look after Frankie, we thought we should give her some helpful tips . . .

SIX REALLY IMPORTANT TIPS FOR ~~BABYSITTING~~ FISH-SITTING A ZOMBIE GOLDFISH:

1. Keep Fang away from Frankie

2. Zombie goldfish only eat green food (mouldy Brussells sprouts, green jelly beans, stinky pond slime)

3. All kittens can be pretty sneaky, but Fang is SUPER sneaky

4. Watch out for Frankie's eyes – he can hypnotise you

5. Did we mention that Fang the vampire kitten is TROUBLE?

6. Seriously, keep Fang away from Frankie!

I think we made our point.

Sami showed right away that she would be a great fish-sitter . . .

when she eventually figured out what she was supposed to do.

She took her fish-sitting responsibilities very seriously.

Sami drew a plan for a Fishy Protection Zone with booby traps to keep out cute evil vampire kittens.

She even added a lookout tower and took it in turns with Frankie to keep watch.

But kittens are sneaky — and Fang is SUPER sneaky, with extra sneaky sprinkles on top.

She is also a master of disguise.

In no time, Fang had managed to sneak
up behind Sami and Frankie and . . .

POUNCE!

Fur flew and fins flailed!

Teeth snapped and tails thwacked!

Claws were bared and green eyes stared!

"Naughty kitty!" Sami shouted.

She put her hands on her hips and used her best cross mum voice.
"Put Frankie down right this instant!"

Just as Sami was about to order Fang to leave,
Fang turned on her special power of kitty cuteness.

Sami was powerless against it.
"I suppose we could all play together," she said.
"I could kitty-sit too!"

Fang and Frankie imagined the fun games they each wanted to play.

Unfortunately, Fang and Frankie found it difficult to play nicely together.

They couldn't agree on a game that didn't end up with somebody being

swooshed,

squashed,

splashed . . .

or ZOMBIFIED.

"If you can't play your games nicely," said Sami,
"then we'll play MY game instead!"

But Sami's game was
NOT their idea of fun.

When Pradeep and I got home, we couldn't believe Fang and
Frankie were playing together! And they were being . . . nice.

We told Sami she was the most fintastic fish-sitter ever! She totally deserved the extra scoops of ice cream we gave her to say thanks.

Maybe cute evil vampire kittens and big fat zombie goldfish CAN get along after all . . .

Well, sometimes.